For Marie-Christine Keith

This is a Borzoi Book published by Alfred A. Knopf, Inc.

Copyright© 1984 by Nicola Bayley
All rights reserved under International and Pan-American Copyright
Conventions. Published in the United States by Alfred A. Knopf, Inc.,
New York. Distributed by Random House, Inc., New York.
Originally published in Great Britain by Walker Books, Ltd.
Manufactured in Italy
2 4 6 8 10 9 7 5 3 1

Library of Congress Cataloging in Publication Data
Bayley, Nicola. Spider cat. (Copycats)
Summary: A cat imagines what it would be like to be a
spider, spinning, eating, and playing in the garden.
[1. Cats – Fiction. 2. Imagination – Fiction.
3. Spiders – Fiction] I. Title. II. Series: Bayley, Nicola.
Copycats. PZ7.B3413Sp 1984 [E] 84-772
ISBN 0-394-86500-6

SPIDER CAT

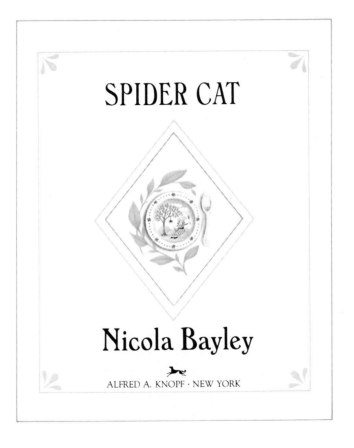

Nicola Bayley

ALFRED A. KNOPF · NEW YORK

If I were a spider
instead of a cat,

I would scurry
to a sunny corner
of the garden,

I would spin
the strongest web
in the world,

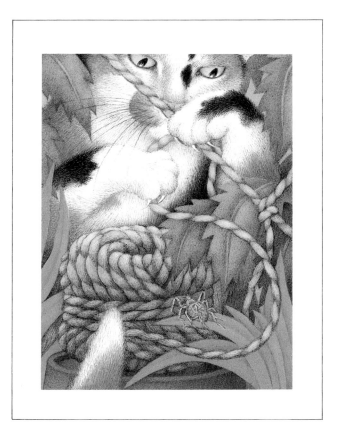

I would catch flies
and eat them
whenever I wanted,

I would blow
in the wind
on a single thread,

I would see
the whole world
sparkling with dew,

and if ever
I were caught
in the pouring rain,

I would quickly
turn back into
a cat again.

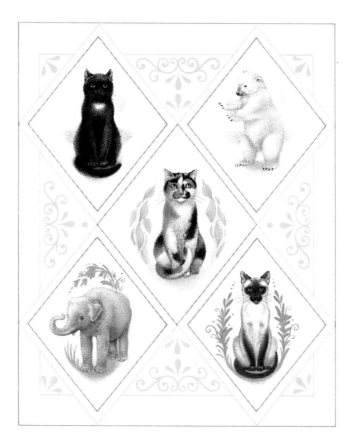